This book belongs to

_____

_____

First published in the UK in 2022
First published in the US in 2022
by Faber and Faber Limited
Bloomsbury House,
74–77 Great Russell Street,
London WC1B 3DA
faberchildrens.co.uk

Text © Lou Kuenzler, 2022
Illustrations © Julia Woolf, 2022
Designed by Faber and Faber
HB ISBN 978–0–571–36181–6
PB ISBN 978–0–571–36182–3

All rights reserved
Printed in India

2 4 6 8 10 9 7 5 3 1

The moral rights of Lou Kuenzler and Julia Woolf
have been asserted

A CIP record for this book is available from the
British Library

MIX
Paper from
responsible sources
FSC
www.fsc.org   FSC® C016779

Faber has published children's books since 1929.
T. S. Eliot's *Old Possum's Book of Practical Cats* and
Ted Hughes' *The Iron Man* were amongst the first. Our
catalogue at the time said that 'it is by reading such
books that children learn the difference between the
shoddy and the genuine'. We still believe in the power
of reading to transform children's lives. All our books
are chosen with the express intention of growing a
love of reading, a thirst for knowledge and to cultivate
empathy. We pride ourselves on responsible editing.
Last but not least, we believe in kind and inclusive books
in which all children feel represented and important.

To the children at Sheldwich Primary.
Thank you for suggesting we should create
a story featuring a robber raccoon!
JW & LK

Lou Kuenzler Julia Woolf

The Robber Raccoon

faber

Rosie Raccoon was up to no good,
out and about in a grand neighbourhood.

With a sack on her back, she crept up to Bear's porch,
then clambered inside by the light of a . . .

. . . torch.

"Wow!" whispered Rosie, eyes wide with surprise, and she snuck away clutching a glittering prize.

"BLAAH!" shrieked the burglar alarm, loud as a horn.

But Rosie had scarpered – off over the lawn.

Into Flamingo's house . . .
one leg off the ground.

"Gracious!" gasped Rosie.
What treasures she'd found!

With her bag full of swag,
it was almost daybreak.

But she couldn't resist
a quick visit to Snake.

CHOC
EGGS

"Stunning!" she sighed, climbing over the sill.
She spotted a trinket which would just fit the bill.

"WHAAH!"

wailed the sirens back down on the street.

But Rosie's crime caper still wasn't complete.

She knew it was wrong as she passed by each door, but she couldn't say no to a few houses . . .

MORE!

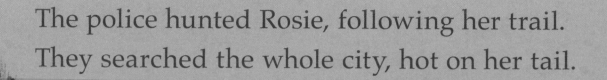

The police hunted Rosie, following her trail.
They searched the whole city, hot on her tail.

"Caught you! You robber!" cried Officer Skunk.
Then he looked at the loot and said, "Hold on, it's . . .

. . . junk!"

Each crime scene was searched by the Sniffer Dog Squad.

They radioed back, saying,

CRIME SCENE

DO NOT ENTER

"This is most odd!

Rosie hasn't robbed jewels or pinched artwork worth millions.

She didn't grab gold or nick banknotes in billions!"

"Of course not!" cried Rosie. "I'm sorry I broke in . . . but I only took litter and things from the bin!"

"You stole useless garbage? How silly," scoffed Bear.

"Exactly!" hissed Snake. "We really don't care."

"Our trash," squawked Flamingo, "isn't worth any money!

You're the worst burglar ever. It's really quite funny."

"You still should have asked." Officer Skunk shook his head.
"It's a crime to just break in and take things," he said.

Then he smiled, gave a shrug, and set Rosie free.
"Just keep this old garbage. What use can it be?"

"Thank you!" cried Rosie. "Though worthless to you,
I'll recycle these treasures and make something . . .

..... NEW!"